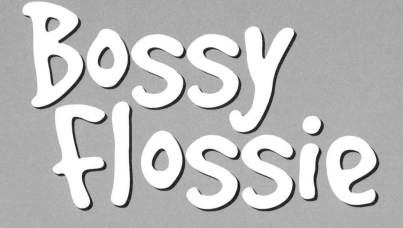

FOR MY GRANDSON
JAMES GREEN
WHO SAID, "DON'T INSULT MY FOOD,"
AND GAVE ME AN IDEA FOR A STORY.
—SG

PENGUIN WORKSHOP
Penguin Young Readers Group
An Imprint of Penguin Random House LLC

Text copyright © 2017 by Sheila Greenwald. Illustrations copyright
© 2017 by Penguin Random House LLC. All rights reserved. Published
by Penguin Workshop, an imprint of Penguin Random House LLC,
345 Hudson Street, New York, New York 10014. PENGUIN and
PENGUIN WORKSHOP are trademarks of Penguin Books Ltd, and
the W colophon is a trademark of Penguin Random House LLC.
Manufactured in China.

Library of Congress Cataloging-in-Publication Data is available.

ISBN 9780448488851 (paperback)   10 9 8 7 6 5 4 3 2 1
ISBN 9780448488868 (library binding)   10 9 8 7 6 5 4 3 2 1

Bossy Flossie

BIZ WHIZ

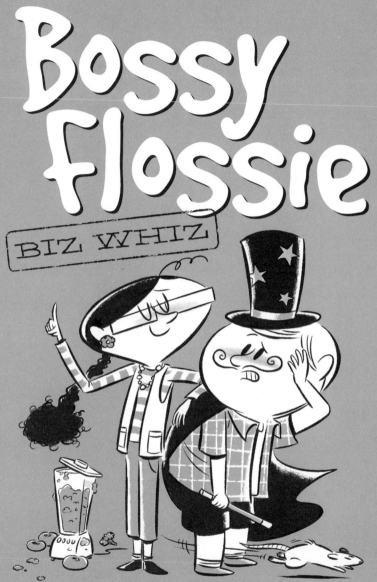

BY SHEILA GREENWALD
ILLUSTRATED BY PIERRE COLLET-DERBY

PENGUIN WORKSHOP ★ AN IMPRINT OF PENGUIN RANDOM HOUSE

1

GREAT NEWS

The first day of school is always my favorite day. I found a mistake on our first-ever third-grade spelling test, corrected two classmates during reading, and explained the proper way to tie a ponytail.

And that was all before lunch.

I thought it couldn't get any better until Ms. Cabot went to the chalkboard and drew a square. At least, that's what I thought it was.

I raised my hand to ask. Good thing I reminded her to explain.

"I have great news," Ms. Cabot announced. "Our class has been chosen to plant a new schoolyard garden."

Everyone looked excited. I was the most excited.

"Even though it's only September now, we can start to think of what we want to grow and of ways to raise money

for our garden tools," Ms. Cabot continued.

"I'll do my lemonade stand or my used-toy sale or haircuts!" I cried out.

I began to *tingle and glow* from head to toe.

Ephraim Thomas giggled. "Who wants a Flossie Popkin haircut?"

"Not me," Imogene Dingle shouted, showing off the Mohawk I gave her by mistake at my beauty parlor.

"But Flossie has a good idea," Ms. Cabot defended me. "A street fair where you could sell lemonade or old toys and books or anything else you want to donate would be a way for us to raise money for our garden. In the next week, I'd like you to form groups to figure out what we could sell at our Street Fair Fundraiser. Each team can have its own table."

"Who wants to be on my team?" I asked.

"Bossy Flossie," Imogene groaned. "Who'd team up with her?"

Everyone laughed except for Gloria Tubbs, who feels sorry for underdogs, and Billy Lark.

Billy was the new boy, and all I had seen him do today was stare out the window. I'm sure he missed

everything that Ms. Cabot said.
I promised myself that I would tell
him later.

I would also tell him that "bossy"
meant I had great ideas and knew
how to make them happen. I'd tell
him he'd be lucky to join my team.

I just worried someone would ask
him first.

BILLY LARK

After the big announcement, we still had to get through a whole science lesson, which was horrible because I already had so many great ideas. Also, I wanted to make sure Billy would be the first member of the Best Team Ever for the Street Fair Fundraiser.

When we finally went to lunch, I made sure to follow Billy so I could be the first person to ask him to join a team.

Of course everyone wanted to be Billy's friend. Ephraim sat next to him at the lunch table. Charlie Diaz even offered him some of his potato chips.

But Billy said no.

"I don't eat junk," he told Charlie.

I stopped worrying. I had a feeling no one would want to team up with him now. Maybe I didn't, either.

"Cabbage Head," Charlie teased, poking at Billy's lunch box full of vegetables.

"Just try a cherry tomato from our garden upstate, and you'll see what I mean," Billy offered, holding out a bag.

"No thanks," Charlie said, shaking his head. "They could be poisoned."

Right away, I knew it wasn't the tomatoes Charlie thought could be poison. It was Billy Lark.

On the way home from school, I tried to catch up with Imogene and Gloria.

"If you let me team up with you, I'll give you great ideas," I told them.

"No way," Imogene said.

Gloria nudged her gently.

"Like what?" Gloria asked.

I thought for a second. And then, lightbulb!

"Cut stems off houseplants, put them in water till they root, then plant them in pots of dirt, and you've got a plant sale."

"That is a *perfect ten*," gushed Gloria, who likes to rate everything from one to ten. "I'd set my mom's begonias in little clay pots with ribbons and bows tied around the bottom to make them prettier."

"Forget clay pots," I said. "Plastic is better. Ribbons and bows are another bad idea. I've tried them before. They get grubby and pathetic."

Gloria's smile faded.

"Selling old stuff on the street is grubby and pathetic," Imogene snapped.

"My Great-Grandpa Morris sold old stuff on the street and ended up owning a department store," I bragged.

"Was his popularity at one out of ten?" Imogene asked.

"No!" I cried. "Everybody loved him. He had loads of friends."

"Then he didn't insult their ideas and the things they liked," Gloria advised softly. "Friends don't do that."

"On a scale of one to ten, Bossy Flossie, your popularity just went from one to zero," Imogene called over her shoulder as she and Gloria hurried off down the street.

Neither of them said good-bye.

I guessed I wouldn't be joining their team.

I'M INVITED

Y ou've been invited," my brother
Simon the science whiz
said when he came home.
He handed me a note that had been
slipped under the door.

Hi Flossie,
Remember me? I moved into
your building last week and I'm
in your class.

I hope it's not too late to ask,
but could you come to dinner at 6
so we can get to know each
other better?

Billy, 15A

"We should be inviting *him*, since he just moved in," Mom said.

I tried to imagine it.

Hungry? Come check out our fridge. Eat what you find. Any time.

Flossie Popkin, 9C.

I read Mom my imaginary note.

"Sorry, Flossie," Mom said. "But you know my late shift at the hospital makes it hard for me to cook the way I used to."

"You mean when our oven was for

baking pies instead of storing used shopping bags?" I asked.

"Someday I'll cook again," Mom promised. She put her coat on over her nurse's uniform and gave me a kiss good-bye. "Don't start any new businesses while I'm gone. And enjoy dinner in 15A, you lucky girl."

Lucky? Me? Why not?

My beauty parlor hadn't worked out, but my lemonade stand and old-toy sales were a success. If I could come up with a great idea for the Street Fair Fundraiser, people would definitely jump at a chance to join my team. I would have to turn them away because Ms. Cabot wouldn't like it if our *whole class* was on my team.

After Mom left, I went to the
kitchen, where Simon was finishing
off a bag of chips.

Inside the fridge, I found food
for his two pet rats, Mr. Salt and
Mr. Pepper, and some smelly leftover
tacos.

I pulled the tacos out of the fridge.

"I wouldn't touch those, if I were you," Simon said, shaking his head. "Toxic tacos!"

As I flipped the tacos into the garbage, I realized that dinner at Billy's was the safest option for me that night.

AN IDEA

B illy is so glad you could come," Mrs. Lark greeted me when she opened the door.

Was that why they had to drag him out of his room?

"We hope you'll like pasta with Billy's homemade tomato sauce and greens fresh from our garden," Mr. Lark said, filling my plate.

"Yummy, yum!" I told him as soon as I could swallow.

Billy didn't say a word, but Mrs. Lark cheered.

"Wonderful!" she cried. "These days, people are so used to food drowning in HFCS that they can't enjoy anything without it."

"I don't even know what an HFCS is," I was happy to let her know. "But I'm sure this tastes better."

"Billy can tell you," his father said.

"High-fructose corn syrup is a fake super sweet that they say makes lab rats blow up to twice the size of ones eating plain sugar," Billy mumbled.

"Billy knows all about healthy food and how to prepare it," his mother boasted. "He made this sauce from our very own cherry tomatoes."

"He heated the tomatoes in oil till they burst and then added cheese to melt in at the end," his father said. "Even though he's not allowed to use the stove by himself yet, he's a real chef."

Billy's ears turned as red as the tomato sauce. "We had such a huge crop this year," his mother went on. "Our carrots were a foot long, and our cabbages were as big as your head."

When Billy stopped eating and pushed away his plate, I wasn't surprised. If I were called Cabbage Head on the first day at a new school, I'd never want to hear the word *cabbage* again.

After dinner, Billy walked me to the door.

"Thanks for asking me to dinner," I said.

"I didn't," he admitted. "When Mom found out everyone called me Cabbage Head because of my lunch, she thought I needed a friend."

"It wasn't because of your lunch you're called Cabbage Head," I informed him. "It's because you insulted *ours*."

"I was trying to be friendly."

"To be friendly, tell us that you like what we like, and leave the veggies at home."

"Now I know why they call you Bossy Flossie," he grumbled.

"What's wrong with being bossy?"
I asked. "It just means I have great
ideas and know how to make them
happen. I'm only trying to help you."

"How does it help if I leave veggies
at home? Mom says we have so much,
we should give them away to a farm
stand."

"Give them to a farm stand?"
I repeated.

Suddenly I began to *tingle and
glow* from head to toe.

"Billy Lark," I said. "Tomorrow, let's talk."

As the elevator carried me down to my floor, I realized maybe my mother was right.

I was a lucky girl.

LUCKY GIRL

The next morning, Ms. Cabot asked us what vegetables we would like to grow in the school garden.

Billy waved his hand in the air.

"Potato chips are ripe all year round," he called out.

When everyone laughed, I was thrilled. Maybe Billy thought I was bossy, but he'd taken my advice.

But later, after he announced

he forgot his lunch, I wondered if he was going too far.

"Try this," Gloria said, offering him half her peanut butter sandwich. "On a scale of one to ten, it's a seven."

"It's a ten," Billy said after one bite. "Best thing I ever ate."

"Then you never tried a Little Libby brownie," Ephraim told him.

"Little Libbys don't compare to Bozos," Charlie argued, adding one to Billy's heap of junk snacks. He gave everything he ate a ten out of ten.

By the time lunch was over, Billy had collected five treats and an invitation to Daisy Wilcox's birthday party.

"This year my dad is buying the top party package from Perfect Parties," Daisy bragged to Billy. "It includes a magician and the best buttercream cake in the world. I hope you can come."

Since he was suddenly so popular, I hoped Billy would remember it was *my* advice that did the trick. I hoped no one would ask him to be on their team before I had a chance.

I was happy when we walked home from school together so we could finally talk. Since Gloria and Imogene didn't want to be on my team, Billy and I could be the best team ever.

"You can't pretend to keep losing your lunch," I told him right away.

"I know," he said worriedly.

"So why don't we trade lunch every morning?" I asked.

"You would do that?" Billy was amazed.

"Why not? I love your food," I said.
"Also, we could sell those veggies your
mom wants to give away at a farm
stand for the street fair."

"A farm stand?" Billy burst out
laughing. "That's wacky."

"Wacky?" I cried. "Meet me in
the lobby in half an hour with a few

bags of vegetables, and I'll prove you're wrong."

As soon as I got home, I found the folding table, money box, and price stickers from my lemonade stand. I pulled out plastic and paper shopping bags from the oven. Also, I took leftover stuffed toys from my last sale in case Billy didn't show up.

But he was waiting for me with two bags full of veggies and a piece of paper he asked me to sign.

○ Farm Stand Contract:
Billy and Flossie Farm Stand

Partner _____   Partner _____

"Partners?" I cried. "I thought we'd be teammates."

Billy looked at my folding table, shopping bags, and money box.

"Not yet," he said. "Today we're partners."

"Partners," I repeated. I began to *tingle and glow* from head to toe. "My Great-Grandpa Morris said,

'Never make a friend a partner; make a partner your friend,'" I told Billy.

"So you mean it's good we aren't friends?"

That wasn't what I meant.

"I meant I never had a partner who could become a friend," I hinted.

"You never had free food to sell, either," Billy said. "Though I don't know who'll buy plain old veggies you can find on any street corner cart."

"They won't be 'plain old' by the time I'm done with them," I assured him.

When he saw how I set Bobby Bear in a forest of broccoli and Funny Bunny holding carrots with Ducky Doodle on a blueberry lake, he agreed.

"But it would be better to tell
how the vegetables are organic and
hand-picked," he said.

"My great-grandpa told me,
'It's presentation that attracts the
public,'" I insisted.

Right away our stand attracted
the public . . . as an art project.

"No one should eat that," said
Mrs. Farnsworth from apartment 7B.

"Didn't anyone tell you not to play
with food?" Mr. Dobbins lectured.

After an hour, a chilly wind blew
from the river.

I folded up my table and put the
shopping bags and money box in
a tote bag.

"You can keep the veggies," Billy said. "Our fridge is stuffed. I've made enough tomato sauce, bean dip, and pesto to fill the freezer. My parents were right. No one cooks anymore. They just want ready-to-eat."

He took the contract out of his pocket and began to crumple it up.

"Don't do that!" I cried. "We're about to grow."

"Grow into what?"

I began to *tingle and glow* from head to toe. "Ready-to-eat."

"Ready-to-eat what?"

"Tomato sauce, bean dip, and pesto. Those would be great things to sell at the street fair."

"But I'm not allowed to use the

stove unless Mom or Dad are around," Billy reminded me. "I can only do a few things on my own."

"A few things are all we need for our Billy and Flossie Ready-to-Eat Treats at the Street Fair Fundraiser."

"The farm stand was a flop," Billy reminded me. "Why don't you give up on a food stand?"

I didn't tell him it wasn't a food stand that I couldn't give up. It was a partner and teammate.

READY-TO-EAT

Upstairs, my brother was looking through takeout menus.

"Chinese or Mexican?" he asked.

"Heat up some oil in a pan. I'll tell you how to make Billy Lark's tomato sauce with pasta," I said.

While Simon boiled pasta, I told him to cook the cherry tomatoes in oil till they burst, and then cut in cheese to melt.

By the time Mom and Dad came home from their hospital shifts, we had the table set for a sit-down dinner.

"This sauce is delicious!" Mom exclaimed. "What do you call it?"

"I call it practice," I said.

"Practice for what?" Dad asked.

"Never mind," I said.

Mom put down her fork. "Let me remind you. You're too young to use the stove."

"But I'm not," Simon piped up. "Cooking is fun."

"Healthy, too," I added. "This sauce has no high-fructose corn syrup that research says makes lab rats blow up to twice the size of ones eating regular sugar."

This time Simon put down his fork.

"That's a great idea for a research paper for the science expo."

We all stared at him.

"Well, I'm not going to actually feed sugar and high-fructose corn syrup to my rats. They're my pets!" Simon said. "But I'm sure there is other research I can gather."

We all agreed, and Simon took a second helping of pasta. "Awesome!" he said.

Awesome was right.

With Simon to cook and Billy to supply veggies and recipes, I'd show him our Street Fair Fundraiser team would be the best.

AWESOME

The next morning, everyone was talking about our garden.

"On a scale of one to ten, this schoolyard garden is going to be a ten!" Gloria exclaimed.

"Growing food to eat is like a miracle," Daisy Wilcox agreed. "I can hardly wait."

"Who cares about vegetables? *I* can hardly wait till Saturday for the best buttercream cake in the world at your birthday," Billy said.

Daisy shook her head sadly. "Last night my dad told me he can't afford the top party package from Perfect Parties. So that means no magician and, even worse, no world's best buttercream cake."

I began to *tingle and glow* from head to toe.

"We can't promise the world's best buttercream cake," I began in a rush.

"But Billy and Flossie's Ready-to-Eat could cater your party for free."

"We could *W-WHAT*?" Billy sputtered.

"Why would you cater a party for free?" Gloria asked.

"It's called promotion," I explained. "A good way to show off our menu before the Street Fair Fundraiser."

"Also a good way to get invited to Daisy's birthday," Imogene mumbled.

"If Dad saves enough on a cake and food, maybe he'd spring for a magician or even a clown," Daisy said. "I'd love a live show."

"We'll do a live show, too," I offered.

"We'll *do w-what*?" Billy sputtered again. His sputtering turned into a coughing fit.

"Food *and* a live show?" Daisy's face lit up. "I'll let you know."

Later, on the way home from school, Billy was angry.

"I'm your partner," he told me. "You should have asked me before you took on a job."

"I thought you would be happy," I explained. "It's an opportunity to

show off your great bean dip before
the Street Fair Fundraiser."

"My *mom* says it's a great bean dip.
It could be awful."

"I've got a can of beans on the shelf
in our kitchen," I remembered. "Come
make some, and we'll know for sure."

"I bet it's awful," Billy warned as I
pulled him off the elevator at my floor.

"Great-Grandpa Morris said,
'Believe in your product and believe
in yourself,'" I lectured.

In the kitchen we found the can
of beans and my brother, Simon. He
was lining two cages with shredded
paper.

"Pet rats!" Billy cried in delight
when he saw them.

He was so excited about Simon's
rats, I had to remind him to show me
how to make bean dip.

"It's just three easy steps," Billy
instructed us. "Watch!"

"Step one: Place beans in blender.

"Step two: Add salt, pepper, and fresh or dried basil.

"Step three: Add oil."

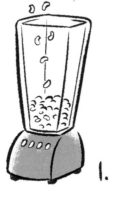

1.

2.

3.

"So far, so good!" I exclaimed.

Billy smiled. "Step four," he said with pride and switched on the blender.

"That's step five," I corrected him. "Step four is put a lid on top."

51

"This dip is delicious," Simon
approved, taking a taste off his
nose.

"Super delicious," I agreed,
scooping some off the sink. "On
Gloria's scale, it's a ten."

Billy blushed and beamed. I had
a feeling he was *tingling and glowing*
from head to toe.

"With the flick of a switch, you created something fantastic," Simon complimented him. "You're a magician with food."

"When people sample this, our phone will ring with orders," I assured Billy.

Just then, the phone actually rang. It was Daisy.

"Mom says no way can you cater my party," she said.

Billy sighed with relief when he heard the news.

But I began to *tingle and glow* from head to toe . . .

"Food wasn't the only thing we offered Daisy for her party," I reminded Billy. "We offered entertainment. I say we have a magic show to put on!"

8

SHOW BIZ

When we met in the lobby of our building the next morning to exchange lunches, Billy informed me that we did not have a show to put on.

"I have no magic act," Billy said.

"You have no confidence," I told him. "I helped you make friends at school. Now I'll help you believe in yourself."

"I believe I'm not a magician."

"Simon called you a magician with food," I reminded him.

"Do I look like a magician?"

"You will when you put on my magician costume from last Halloween."

"*Last* Halloween's costume will be too small," Billy said.

"Simon's costume won't be," I said. "It includes a mustache, a wand, and a trick hat with a secret compartment."

"A mustache, a trick hat, and a wand?" Billy nodded slowly. "Okay, I'll try it on."

At school, I let Daisy know we had a magic act.

"Even though you don't want our food, I haven't forgotten the live show I promised. We've got one you will never forget."

"Like my haircut?" Imogene called out, pulling on the frizz that was growing in over her ears.

"It's hard to make curly hair the same on both sides," I admitted. "Magic is easier. This time there won't be any mistakes."

At lunchtime everyone wanted to know what our show would be.

"Can Billy pull a rabbit out of a hat?" Charlie teased.

"Better than that," I said.

As we walked home, Billy wanted to know what would go in the magic hat.

"Funny Bunny," I said.

"Funny Bunny is *stuffed*," Billy replied.

"Great-Grandpa said . . ."

"I know what he said," Billy interrupted. "He said believe in your product. He said it's all about presentation, but what did he say about flops?"

"He said flops are how you learn to succeed."

"What did you learn from Ready-to-Eat and the farm stand?"

"I learned we should have been better prepared. We should have had a menu and good signs. We weren't ready. This time I made a list."

Posters! Costumes! Rehearsals!

As soon as we got home, we went to work.

"Maybe I believe in magic," Billy said.

By late afternoon on Friday, we were ready for a dress rehearsal.

Mom and Dad and Simon shouted, "Bravo!" Mrs. Lark said she would cut veggie sticks to scoop up dip from the magic blender act. Mr. Lark thought we should be on TV.

When Billy pulled Funny Bunny out of his hat, everyone laughed.

"Funnier than a real rabbit," Mom cried. "Your show has everything."

But just before he went home, Billy told me, "Our show doesn't have *everything*. Funny Bunny made everyone laugh with surprise. Magic should make them gasp in amazement."

After Billy left, I thought about what he had said.

I needed to come up with something that would make people gasp in amazement.

I tried and I tried.

Some ideas were amazing, but
they wouldn't cause a gasp.

Some ideas would cause a gasp,
but they weren't amazing.

I got so tired thinking up ideas,
I fell asleep . . . and dreamed.

When I woke up, I knew exactly
how to make everyone gasp in
amazement—even Billy.

Saturday morning, Simon waited
while we put on our costumes and

loaded the shopping cart with a
blender and food for our act.

"Why are you taking *your* magician
hat?" Billy asked.

"For good luck," I lied, tucking it
carefully into its box.

Before Mom and Dad left for work,
Dad took photos of us.

"Now our show really has
everything," I told Billy. "It's time to
take it on the road."

ON THE ROAD

At Daisy's, a long table was set with paper plates and party poppers and goody bags. There was a layer cake I'd seen on a turntable in the window at the corner deli. It was covered with sugar roses. There were cups of soda and cider and glasses of milk. There were balloons and streamers.

After we ate cake and ice cream, the table was cleared for our show.

I plugged in the blender and set
out containers of beans, herbs, oil,
and spices. Then I passed around
Mrs. Lark's platter of cut-up carrots,

sugar snap peas, celery, and lettuce leaves to scoop the dip.

When I was finished, I clapped my hands for attention.

"Billy and his magic blender will turn these simple items into something you will never forget," I told the audience.

Billy waved his wand while I dumped everything into the blender.

"Abracadabra," Billy said. I put the lid on top and pressed the switch.

"Abracadabra?" Imogene hooted. "You're just making stuff with a blender. That's not magic."

I spooned the dip into a bowl and passed it around so everyone could scoop with veggie sticks for a taste.

"Yummy," Mrs. Wilcox approved.

Maybe they didn't think it was magic, but that didn't stop everyone from gobbling up the dip.

"Do you have any real tricks?" Daisy called out.

"Yeah, pull a rabbit out of that hat," Ephraim teased.

"He can't pull anything out of the hat," Charlie said.

I clapped again.

Billy bowed and took off his hat.

Everyone grew very quiet when he showed how the inside was empty.

Then he closed his eyes, reached a hand inside the brim, and pulled out Funny Bunny.

"A stuffed rabbit?" Daisy shouted. "That's not magic."

"It's dumber than the dip," Charlie taunted.

Everyone began to boo.

Billy's face got so red that he
looked as if he was about to melt.

"Oops, wrong hat," I cried, taking
mine from its box and handing it to
Billy.

"What's in this one?" he
whispered. "Ducky Doodle?"

I clapped my hands again for
attention.

"You are about to see something more amazing than anything you ever saw before," I announced.

Billy reached inside my hat and held up what he found inside.

EVERYONE GASPED IN AMAZEMENT.

Then Mrs. Wilcox screamed.

Mr. Wilcox said, "What is that?"

And Mrs. Wilcox screamed back, "What do you think it is?"

And Daisy screamed . . .

"A rat!"

"Not just any rat!" I shouted above the screaming. "That's Mr. Salt." I wanted to explain more, but Mr. Salt wriggled out of Billy's hand and scampered on the floor. Everyone began to scream even louder.

Billy put his hands over his ears and closed his eyes.

Some kids climbed up on their chairs. Others fell off their chairs.

Then Mr. Wilcox caught Mr. Salt. Mrs. Wilcox banged two pots together for attention.

"Take that thing away," she shouted at me and Billy. "Call someone to come pick you up. *Right now!*"

SORRY

I'm sorry," I told Billy while we waited for my brother in Daisy's lobby.

"*You're* sorry," he stormed. "I'm sorry I ever gave you veggies in return for lunch. I'm sorry I ever went along with all your wacky ideas and flops."

"My Great-Grandpa Morris said flops are the road to success. He said you should shoot for the moon and even if you miss, you could land

among the stars. He said success is how high you bounce after you hit bottom."

"I'm not bouncing," Billy said.

By the time my brother arrived to pick us up, I wasn't bouncing anymore, either.

Simon was angry.

"I never gave you permission to take Mr. Salt out of the house," he scolded.

As soon as I got home, I went to my room and crawled into bed. Before I knew it, my eyes were faucets that only turned off in sleep.

When I woke up, Dad was tapping on my door.

"Mom's cooked a delicious stew with the vegetables you brought home from your farm stand," he whispered. "And she baked a pie with the blueberries."

In the dining room, the table was set. Simon was sitting in one of the chairs. He didn't look so angry anymore.

"Even if I'm on the late shift, I can prepare dinners and freeze them for the week ahead," Mom said. "Thanks to you, Flossie, I've been inspired to cook again."

"Thanks to you, Simon was inspired to research HFCS," Dad said.

Simon smiled a little.

"So maybe your ideas were a success after all," Mom said.

If they were such a success, how come I didn't feel like eating?

Instead I called Daisy.

"I'm sorry I ruined your party," I apologized.

"Me too. The tricks were stupid, and the rat was beyond horrible."

"Was there anything good about it?" I asked.

"Let me think." Daisy paused.
"My mom loved those veggies."

Then I scribbled an apology note
to Simon.

Dear Simon,

Sorry for taking Mr. Salt.
I won't do it again. Promise.

Your sister, Flossie

Finally, I called Billy.

"So do I get to keep the hat and
cape and wand and mustache?"
he asked.

"What for?"

"You never know."

"I know my ideas for the Street Fair Fundraiser all flopped," I said. "I know no one will join my team."

I began to cry.

"I know I should have told you what was in the hat. I should have listened to you and shared ideas since you're my partner. I know because of me, we were a *total* and complete failure."

"Total and complete?" Billy repeated.

"Except Mrs. Wilcox loved the veggies."

"Okay." Billy sounded relieved. "So maybe we're about to grow."

"Grow into what?"

"A farm stand where Mrs. Wilcox can find the veggies she loves at the Street Fair Fundraiser."

"But our farm stand flopped, too."

"That's because you wouldn't listen to me and used your stuffed animals as decorations. This time *I'll* make signs telling how our food is organic and hand-picked."

"*You'll* make signs? You said you

were sorry you ever partnered with me."

"I changed my mind. We have a contract," Billy said.

"Throw it away."

"It's not just the contract," Billy told me. "Charlie and Ephraim thought the rat was awesome. They want to be on our team."

"Awesome? *Our* team?" I stopped crying. "Charlie and Ephraim?"

"Next weekend, we'll be picking apples and pears up at our farm. Maybe you'd like to come and help out."

"You're inviting *me*?" I couldn't believe it. "For the weekend?"

"Remember what your great-grandpa said about partners?" Billy asked.

"Never make a friend your partner . . . ," I started to say.

"Make your partner a friend," Billy concluded.

All of a sudden I began to *tingle and glow* from head to toe.

It wasn't because I had a new idea for the Street Fair Fundraiser. Even if selling apples and pears was a flop, I knew it would still be the best idea I ever dreamed of.

I had a partner who was a friend.

Suddenly I was hungry.

BILLY'S BEANS

(Ask an adult for help with the blender.) Put into the blender:

> 1 can white beans, drained
>
> 1/4 cup olive oil
>
> Salt and pepper to taste
>
> 1 clove garlic
>
> 1/4 cup fresh parsley

Blend till smooth.

Scoop up with carrot or celery sticks.

BILLY'S CHERRY TOMATO SAUCE

·····································

1 tablespoon olive oil

1 pint cherry tomatoes

1 tablespoon olive oil

1 clove garlic, minced

Salt and pepper to taste

1/4 cup or more mozzarella
   cheese, cubed

1/4 cup fresh parsley or basil,
   or 1 teaspoon each, dried

Heat oil in pan (ask an adult for
help with the stove), add tomatoes,
and heat till they begin to burst.

Mash them with a fork.

Add garlic, salt, and pepper, and cook till garlic softens.

Add cheese, and heat till it melts into the sauce.

Add parsley or basil, and serve over pasta.